MOLLY MARCHES ON

BY VALERIE TRIPP

ILLUSTRATIONS NICK BACKES

VIGNETTES SUSAN MCALILEY

THE AMERICAN GIRLS COLLECTION®

Published by Pleasant Company Publications
Previously published in *American Girl*® magazine

For information, address: Book Editor, Pleasant Company Publications, 8400 Fairway Place, P.O. Box 620998, Middleton, WI 53562.

Printed in Singapore.
01 02 03 04 05 06 07 08 TWP 10 9 8 7 6 5 4 3 2 1

Edited by Nancy Holyoke and Michelle Jones
Designed by Joshua Mjaanes and Laura Moberly
Art Directed by Katie Brown and Joshua Mjaanes

Library of Congress Cataloging-in-Publication Data

Tripp, Valerie, 1951-
Molly marches on / by Valerie Tripp ;
illustrations, Nick Backes ; vignettes, Susan McAliley.
p. cm. — (The American girls collection)
Summary: Molly is sure that she will find the surprise at the end of the overnight nature hike at Camp Gowonagin, but then she finds her own secret surprise.

ISBN 1-58485-276-3
[1. Camps—Fiction.] I. Backes, Nick, ill. II. McAliley, Susan, ill.
III. Title. IV. Series.
PZ7.T7363 Moak 2001 [Fic]—dc21 00-032638

OTHER AMERICAN GIRLS
SHORT STORIES:

FELICITY TAKES A DARE

JOSEFINA'S SONG

KIRSTEN SNOWBOUND!

ADDY'S WEDDING QUILT

SAMANTHA AND THE
MISSING PEARLS

Picture Credits

The following individuals and organizations have generously given permission to reprint illustrations contained in "Looking Back": p. 30—National Museum of American History, Smithsonian Institution; p. 31—Illustration by Laszlo Kubinyi; p. 33—Joslyn Art Museum, Omaha, NE; p. 34—Courtesy of Lewis & Clark Interpretive Center, Washburn, ND; p. 35—Missouri Historical Society, St. Louis; p. 36—From the collection of Gilcrease Museum, Tulsa, OK, *Elk Hide Painting* by Unidentified Artist, 8926.140 (detail); p. 37—W. T. Richards; pp. 38–39—The Ewell Sale Stewart Library, The Academy of Natural Sciences; p. 40—© Charles Mauzy/CORBIS; p. 41—State Historical Society of North Dakota, C1106 Sakakawea Statue, Capitol Grounds, Bismarck, ND; p. 42—Photography by Jamie Young and prop styling by Jean doPico.

Table of Contents

DAD
Molly's father, a doctor who is somewhere in England, taking care of wounded soldiers.

MOM
Molly's mother, who holds the family together while Dad is away.

MOLLY
A ten-year-old who is growing up on the home front in America during World War Two.

JILL
Molly's fifteen-year-old sister, who is always trying to act grown-up.

RICKY
Molly's thirteen-year-old brother—a big pest.

BRAD
Molly's six-year-old brother—a little pest.

LINDA
One of Molly's best friends, a practical schemer.

SUSAN
Molly's other best friend, a cheerful dreamer.

MISS BUTTERNUT
The counselor at Camp Gowonagin.

MOLLY MARCHES ON

Molly McIntire ran up the path to her tent as fast as her legs could carry her. She flung back the tent flap and announced, "We're going! Tomorrow's the day! All the new campers are going on the overnight nature hike!"

"Hurray!" shrieked Linda and Susan, Molly's best friends, who were also new campers.

"You lucky ducks," sighed their tent-mate Irene. She had been at camp before, so she was an old camper. "I wish I could go on that hike again."

"I can't wait!" exclaimed Molly. Ever since she had arrived at Camp Gowonagin one week ago, the old campers had been telling her about the overnight nature hike. It was the first hike of the summer, so that alone made it exciting. But what made it extra special was this: there was a surprise at the end. Old campers were sworn to secrecy about it. "We can't tell you what the surprise is," they'd say. "But, oh! You'll love it!"

Molly often daydreamed about what the surprise might be. A cave? A lake? An eagle's nest? To Molly the surprise was all the more wonderful because you had to earn it. It was a discovery to be found only at the end of a long, hard hike. No one was going to give the surprise away, so Molly didn't ask questions about it. She was enchanted with the mystery of it all.

But Linda liked to get to the bottom of things. "This surprise business is for the birds," she was saying to Irene. "Couldn't you at least give us a hint?"

Irene just grinned.

"I hope it doesn't have to do with canoes," said Susan nervously. "We don't have to paddle up a waterfall or anything, do we?"

Irene giggled. "I can't tell you what the surprise is," she said. "But, oh! You'll love it."

Molly was sure she would.

In fact, Molly was sure she was going to love the whole overnight nature hike more than any other girl at Camp Gowonagin. She had been looking forward to being in the woods for so long! Back home, before she came to camp, Molly had read a book about Sacagawea, the Shoshone Indian woman who helped the explorers Lewis and Clark on their journey through the wilderness, across the Rocky Mountains, and to the Pacific Ocean in 1805. Molly thought Sacagawea was the bravest, smartest, most admirable person she had ever heard of.

On the nature hike, I will be just like

Sacagawea, Molly thought as she packed her rucksack. *I'll walk silently through the woods. I'll sleep under the stars. I'll cook over a campfire. And when I reach the surprise, I'll be just like Sacagawea finding the Pacific Ocean with Lewis and Clark. Oh, if Sacagawea could see me tomorrow, I know she'd be proud!*

"We're from Gowonagin, and no one could be prouder, and if you cannot hear us, we'll yell a little louder!"

"Louder?" muttered Molly crossly. Ever since they'd left camp at sunrise that morning, all the other hikers had been yowling stupid songs at the top of their lungs. They screeched at vincs that looked like snakes. They stamped on sticks to snap them.

Everyone, including her own friends Linda and Susan, was ruining the nature hike for Molly. They were *supposed* to be moving silently, swiftly through the woods, without disturbing so much as a leaf. Instead, they were crashing through the woods like a herd of stampeding elephants! Molly knew this was not the way true woodspeople conducted themselves. She was sure Sacagawea would be horrified.

Even Miss Butternut, the counselor who was leading the hike, was acting all wrong. She tooted on her bugle to get the girls' attention, and then she began speaking in her loud fluty voice as if they

Everyone was ruining the nature hike for Molly. They were ***supposed*** *to be moving silently, swiftly through the woods.*

were all back in the Mess Hall at camp!

"Girls," she said. "Observe these stones placed in the shape of an arrowhead. These stones point out our way." A little later she asked, "Girls, can anyone tell me what this stick supported by two other sticks means?"

Susan, whose sister was a Girl Scout, piped up with the answer. "That means it's two more miles to the end of the trail," she said.

"Splendid, Susan!" Miss Butternut said, beaming. "Now, girls, do you see the berry stain on the trunk of this tree?"

Molly didn't pay much attention while Miss Butternut talked loudly on and on about different trail marks. Molly thought sticks and stones and berry juice on trees were for babies. Sacagawea certainly didn't have any such trail marks to follow in the wilderness. Oh, no! Sacagawea had to rely on the shadows cast by the trees, the scent of water in the air, and the sound of the wind to find *her* way. Molly started to pretend that she was Sacagawea. She took some deep breaths.

"What are you doing?" asked Susan. She and Linda were walking behind Molly.

"I'm smelling the air like Sacagawea did," said Molly.

"What for?" asked Susan.

"To find the way," said Molly shortly.

"You're kidding," said Linda. "That's silly. You can just follow the trail marks, for Pete's sake."

But Susan took a deep breath, too. "Do you smell wienies?" she asked Molly. "I'm sort of hoping the surprise is that someone is cooking lunch for us. I hope it's wienies!"

Linda laughed. "Wienies? That's not what hikers eat." She began to sing, "Great green gobs of greasy grimy gopher guts . . ."

"Cut it out!" said Molly, annoyed. But Linda just sang louder, and soon the other hikers were singing with her. Molly was glad when Miss Butternut blew her bugle and all the hikers stopped singing and came to a halt.

"Well, girls, this is it," said Miss Butternut. "This is where the race to the surprise begins." She waited for the girls' cheers to die down before she went on. "I will now divide you into two teams. Each team has its own marked trail to follow. At the end of your trail, you'll find the surprise. You'll know when you get there because the surprise is . . . well, I can't tell you what it is, but—"

"We'll love it!" all the hikers shouted together.

"Yes!" said Miss Butternut with a laugh. "And lunch is there, too."

Quickly, Miss Butternut divided the hikers into teams. Molly, Linda, and Susan were on a team with five girls they didn't know very well.

"Now, before you go," said Miss

Butternut, "let's recite the three rules of hiking."

Rules! thought Molly. *Sacagawea didn't need rules any more than she needed trail marks.* But all the other girls spoke together: "Never hike alone. Stay on the marked trail. Carry water."

"Splendid!" said Miss Butternut. "Very well, off you go! See you at the surprise."

"Hurray!" the girls yelled as they set forth into the woods.

Molly walked fast so that she was well ahead of the rest of her noisy team. After a short while, she came to a place where the trail split in two. Molly never stopped. She forged ahead on the branch of the trail that led steeply downhill. The rest of the team stopped at the split.

"Hey, Molly!" Linda shouted after her. "You're going the wrong way!"

Molly walked back to the split. "No, I'm not," she said.

"Yes, you are," said Susan. "The trail goes uphill. See that stick pointing the way?"

"That's just an old stick that fell off a tree," said Molly. "Anybody can see that the bigger trail goes downhill. That uphill trail is just a deer path or something."

"No, it's not—" Susan began.

"The trail goes uphill," said Susan. "See that stick pointing the way?"

"Let's not waste time arguing," cut in Linda. "Everyone who wants to go downhill, follow Molly. Everyone who wants to go uphill, follow me."

Molly turned sharply and marched down the steep path. No one followed her.

"You're breaking the first rule of hiking," Susan called after her.

"I don't care!" Molly shouted back. And she didn't. Now at last she could *really* feel like Sacagawea, alone in the quiet woods. Down, down, down Molly walked. She was proud of the way she moved smoothly and placed her feet gently so she did not make any noise.

The trail grew narrower each step of the way. It crossed Molly's mind that they'd hiked uphill all morning, so it was a little funny that she was going steadily downhill now. And she did wish the trail weren't getting so hard to follow. After an hour of hiking alone, she was only guessing where the trail was.

Molly stopped to decide which way to go. She heard a bird whistling, and leaves rustling, and—with shock, Molly heard the thump of heavy footsteps and the crackling sound of a large creature pushing through the underbrush. Molly's heart beat fast. Was it a bear? Was it a bobcat? She looked around frantically for a tree to climb.

"Molleee!" a voice called. "Molly! Where are you?"

Molly let out her breath. That was no bear. That was Susan. "I'm over here!" she shouted.

Susan emerged from the trees, red-faced and sweaty. "I couldn't let you break the first rule of hiking," she panted.

Molly didn't want to admit it, but she was quite glad to see her friend. "How'd you find me?" she asked.

"Gosh, I don't know," said Susan. "I think you must have broken the second rule of hiking, too. That's the one about staying on the marked trail. I haven't seen any trail marks for miles." Susan plopped down on a rock. "I hope you didn't break the third rule of hiking. I hope you brought water. I drank all of mine."

"I have water," said Molly. She searched in her rucksack for her leather water pouch. She'd packed it instead of her metal canteen because she felt the pouch was more like something Sacagawea would have carried. She pulled the pouch out now and discovered that it was empty. The water had leaked out all over everything in her rucksack.

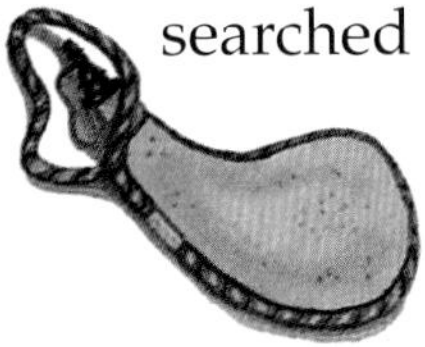

Susan looked at the empty pouch and sighed.

Suddenly Molly felt ashamed. "Oh, Susan," she said. "I'm sorry. I was wrong about the downhill trail. Everyone else is probably already at the surprise. It's bad enough I got myself lost, but now I've got you lost, too. What are we going to do?"

"Well," said Susan with half a grin, "maybe you better smell the air again. Maybe that'll help us find the way."

Molly laughed in spite of herself. She took a deep, noisy breath. Susan giggled. Molly took another exaggerated breath. The odd thing was, Molly really *did* smell something.

"You know what?" she said. "I think I smell water. And I think I hear water, too. Come on."

Molly followed the rushing, gurgling sound through a clump of trees and down a little slope to a small stream.

"Hey!" said Susan. "The Sacagawea stuff worked!"

"Let's follow the stream," suggested Molly. "Maybe it leads to Lake Gowonagin."

"O.K.," said Susan.

The two tired girls followed the stream as it twisted and turned its way through the woods. Then all of a sudden, the trees stopped. The stream had led them to a small clearing at the edge of a beautiful little pond. The pond water was dark, smooth, and peaceful.

"Ooh," breathed Susan and Molly together. Right away both girls sat down, kicked off their shoes, peeled off their socks, and dipped their feet in the cool water. *This is how Sacagawea must have felt when she finally put her feet in the Pacific Ocean,* Molly thought.

This is how Sacagawea must have felt when she finally put her feet in the Pacific Ocean, Molly thought.

Susan spoke in a soft voice. "I wonder if anyone has ever been here before."

"I don't know," said Molly. "Maybe we discovered it."

For a long while, Molly and Susan sat at the edge of the pond without saying a word, just resting and enjoying the feeling of sun on their faces. Then Susan sighed. "I hate to leave," she said. "But we'd better try to find our way back to camp."

Just then Molly heard the unmistakable sound of lots of feet stomping through the woods. "It's Miss Butternut and the girls!" she exclaimed joyfully. She jumped up and yelled, "Yoo-hoo! Over here! It's us!" This time, Molly was very happy to hear the hikers stampeding like a herd of elephants.

She was even more pleased to see them as they appeared through the trees and crowded around her and Susan. Everyone was talking at once.

"Boy, did we have a time finding you!" said Linda. "We thought you were lost forever!"

"So did we!" said Susan.

"Girls!" said Miss Butternut in a voice that made them immediately quiet. Her round face was flushed. She put her hands on her hips and said to Molly and Susan, "Well. And what do you two have to say for yourselves?"

Molly could hardly look Miss Butternut in the eye. "It . . . it was all my fault, Miss Butternut," she said, shamefaced. "Susan just came after me to try to help me. I was the one who broke the rules of hiking. I won't do it again. I'm really sorry."

Miss Butternut shook her head. "The rules of hiking are not to be taken lightly," she said. "I think you've found *that* out."

Molly said, "I sure have."

Miss Butternut put one arm around Molly and the other around Susan. She looked out at the pond for a moment. Then she said, "And you've found something else, too. I've never seen this pond before. It's a beauty! What are you going to name it, girls?"

Molly and Susan looked at each other and smiled. "We'd like to call it

Sacagawea's Pond," said Molly. "Because she helped us find it."

"I am sure Sacagawea would be proud," said Miss Butternut. Then she said to the rest of the campers, "Who'd like a swim?"

"I would!" yelled the girls as they pulled their swimsuits out of their packs.

"Last one in is a rotten egg!" said Miss Butternut.

What a surprising day, thought Molly as she swam out to the middle of the pond. Suddenly she stopped still. The surprise! She had forgotten all about the surprise! "Linda!" she called out to her friend who was floating on her back nearby.

"What?" asked Linda lazily.

"Listen! When Susan and I were lost, did the rest of you find the surprise?"

"Yup," said Linda.

Molly couldn't stand it. "Well, come on! You've got to tell me. What is it? What's the surprise?" she demanded.

Without turning her head, Linda grinned. Right away Molly knew exactly what Linda was going to say, and she knew she deserved it. Sure enough, Linda answered, "I can't tell you what the surprise was. But, oh! You would have loved it!"

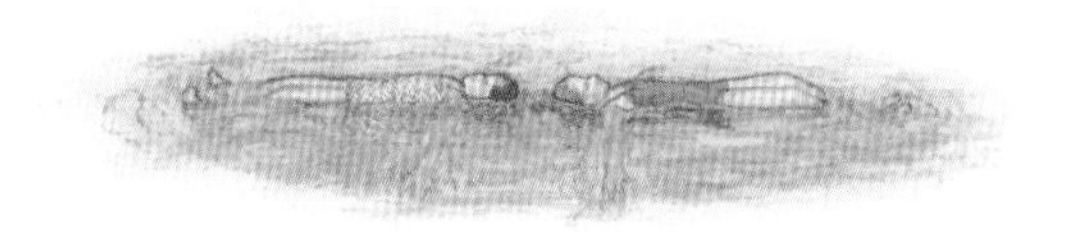

VALERIE TRIPP

At 9 Now

When I was Molly's age, I went to a summer camp just like Camp Gowonagin. I loved the nights when everyone gathered around a big campfire to sing camp songs, roast marshmallows, and listen to the counselors tell stories about Sacagawea.

Valerie Tripp has written thirty-six books in The American Girls Collection, including nine about Molly.

A Peek Into the Past

At summer camp, Molly and her friends learned skills like those the pioneers used. Campers practiced starting a fire and building a shelter with only a blanket and sticks. When campers went on hikes, they learned how to identify birds and trees, read a compass, and follow trail markings. Miss Butternut and other counselors told stories about famous explorers like Lewis and Clark, who charted a trail through the wilderness 140 years before Molly's time.

Lewis and Clark's compass

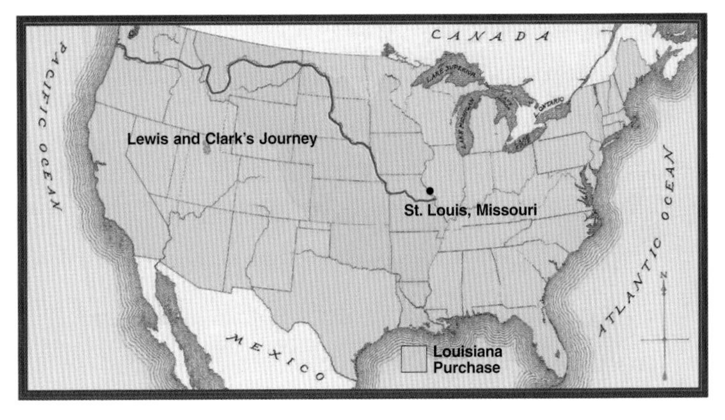

Lewis and Clark traveled from St. Louis, Missouri, all the way to the Pacific Ocean.

President Thomas Jefferson sent Meriwether Lewis and William Clark to explore the Louisiana Territory, the vast lands bought by the United States in 1803. He wanted them to find a passage over the Rocky Mountains to the Pacific Ocean. In October 1804, Lewis and Clark stopped to camp for the winter near a Hidatsa Indian village in what is now

North Dakota. There they met a young woman named Sacagawea (sah-KAH-gah-we-ah).

Sacagawea was a Shoshone Indian who had been captured by the Hidatsas when she was about 12 years old. The Hidatsas gave her the name Sacagawea, or "Bird Woman." When she was 16, she was sold to a French-Canadian fur trader to be his wife.

When Lewis and Clark met Sacagawea, they hired her and her husband to join them on their journey. One reason Lewis and Clark hired them was to translate Indian languages. Sacagawea knew the Hidatsa and Shoshone languages, and her husband knew Hidatsa and French. When

Sacagawea meeting her husband at the Hidatsa Indian camp

the traveling group came upon Shoshone Indians, Sacagawea could translate into Hidatsa for her husband. Then he could translate into French, and someone in Lewis and Clark's group could translate into English—like a game of telephone!

In April 1805, the group set out on their journey. They had one addition—Sacagawea's new baby boy. His father named him Jean-Baptiste, but Clark nicknamed him "Pomp."

In May, Sacagawea helped the group avoid a disaster. The boat she was riding in hit a high wind and nearly capsized. Sacagawea rescued the tools, food and supplies, and medicine chest

A dugout canoe like the one Lewis and Clark used

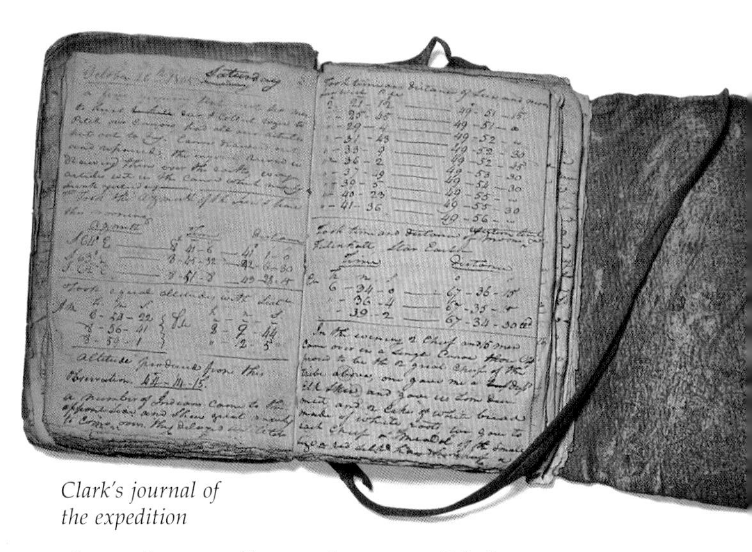

Clark's journal of the expedition

that almost floated away. If the group had lost these items, they would have had to turn back. Both Lewis and Clark wrote in their journals that they were impressed with Sacagawea's bravery and calmness under pressure.

Lewis and Clark knew that to continue their journey across the Rocky Mountains,

A painting of Shoshone horses

they would have to get horses from the Shoshones, Sacagawea's people. Lewis and Clark thought having a Shoshone in their group would help them get the horses they needed. For Sacagawea, this was a chance to see her people for the first time in many years.

In mid-August, the group found the Shoshones. Sacagawea cried with joy! Her brother was their chief. Lewis began

Lewis meeting the Shoshone

bargaining with the Shoshones for the horses, but he found out that the Shoshones were taking all of their horses on a buffalo hunt. Sacagawea talked to her brother and explained that the white men had to have their horses before the winter or their expedition would never make it over the mountains. At last Sacagawea convinced him, and Lewis and Clark got the horses they needed to continue their journey.

That fall, Sacagawea kept the expedition safe when the group traveled through other Indian territories. Some of the Indians had never seen white men before, and they were prepared to defend their lands. But a war party never traveled with an Indian woman and a baby, so when the Indians saw Sacagawea and Pomp, they knew that the group came in peace.

Along the trail, Sacagawea helped the group gather roots and berries for food. She found prairie

Prairie turnip

turnips, wild artichokes, currants, and bitterroot. Lewis collected and pressed many of these plants so scientists could draw and name them.

Bitterroot

In November, the group was within 20 miles of its goal: the Pacific Ocean. A decision needed to be made—camp for the winter or press on to the ocean by foot. Everyone was given a vote in the decision, even Sacagawea. The group decided to set up camp.

By January 1806, Sacagawea had been near the ocean for more than a month and had still not seen it. One day, Clark was organizing a small group to find a whale that was beached on the ocean's shore.

The Pacific Ocean off the Oregon coast

The expedition was running out of food, and the whale meat could help them survive. Sacagawea asked to go along so she could see the great waters for herself. It was the chance of a lifetime.

The end of Sacagawea's story is a mystery. Some say she died in 1812, near where her journey started. Others say she returned to the Shoshones in Wyoming and lived to be nearly 100 years old.

What we do know about Sacagawea is that the country she helped explore did not forget her. Today there are at least three mountains, two lakes, and 23 monuments named for her. It is said that there are more monuments dedicated to Sacagawea than to any other woman in America.

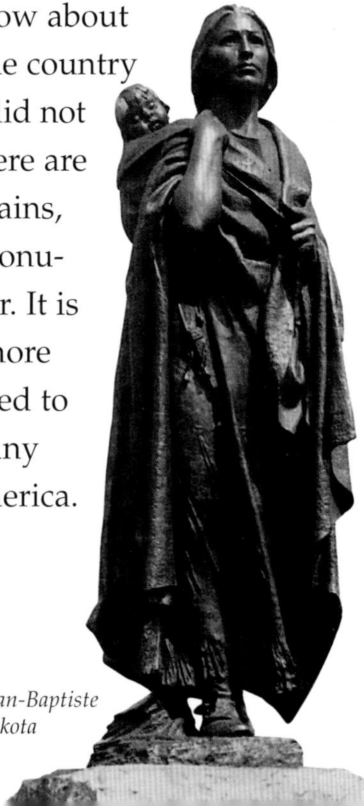

A statue of Sacagawea and Jean-Baptiste in Bismarck, North Dakota

AN
AMERICAN
GIRLS
PASTIME

Track a Trail

Mark a trail, then
follow it with your friends.

At Camp Gowonagin, Molly learned how to follow a trail just as Sacagawea might have done. Molly went hiking without a map, and she marked trails so she could find her way back. She used leaves, twigs, and branches to make signs that all the campers knew how to read.

Learn these signs with your friends, then mark some trails. See if you can follow them!

You Will Need:

*Sticks**

Pebbles

Leaves

**Be sure to use sticks that have fallen to the ground.*

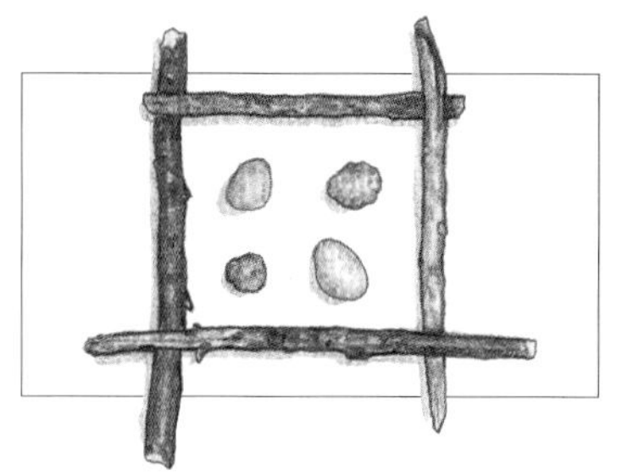

Make a square with 4 sticks. Place one pebble inside the square for each step to take.

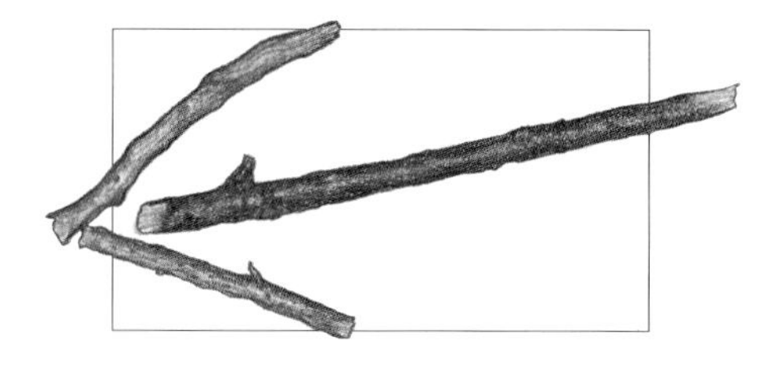

Make an arrow with 3 sticks to show in which direction to head.

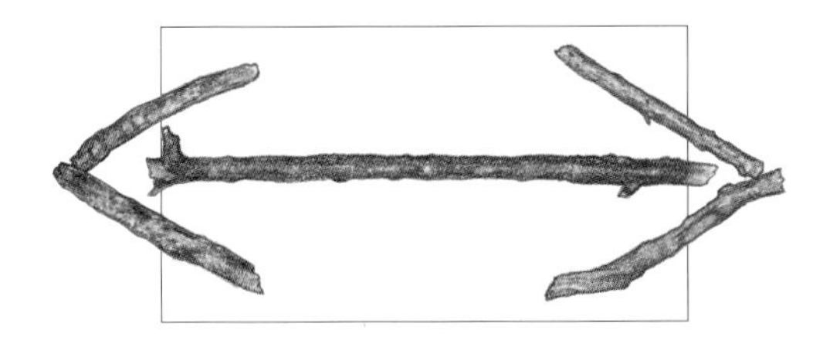

Make a double-ended arrow with 5 sticks to show a turnaround.

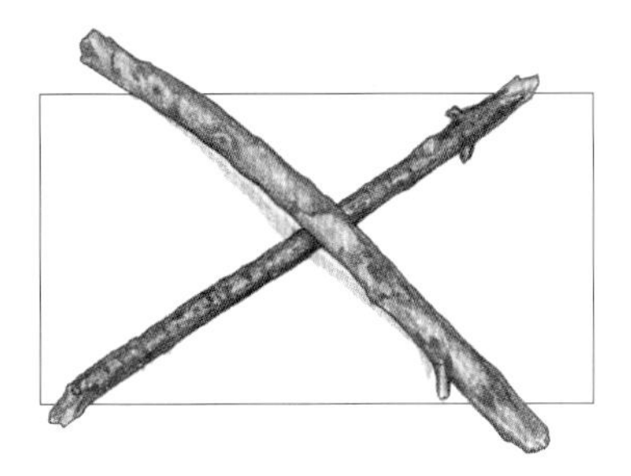

Make an X with 2 sticks to show "wrong way!" This is helpful when a path splits.

Weave a twig into a leaf to show "keep going." This is helpful when the path is very long.

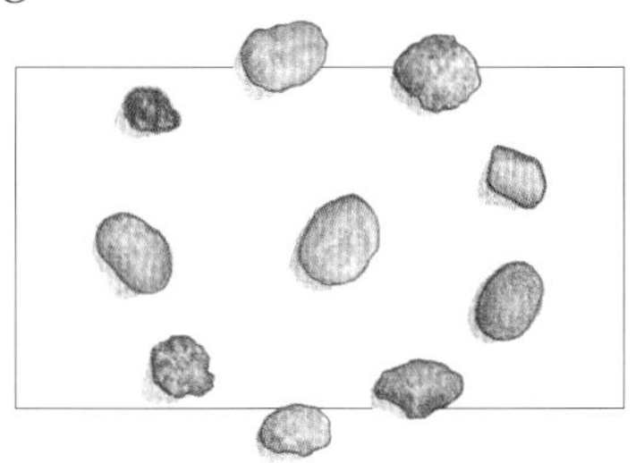

Make a circle out of pebbles. Place one pebble in the middle to show "go home."